Case File: 001

New Kids on the Rock

Mark Miller

MillerWords
PO Box 1622
Mount Dora, FL 32756

Cover design: Paul S. Seus

Third Edition

For discounts on bulk purchases, please contact MillerWords Educational Sales at
Sales@MillerWords.com

Printed in the United States of America

4 6 8 10 9 7 5 3

Library of Congress Control Number: 2015917551

ISBN: 978-0692561027

Read the entire series!

Small World
Global Protection Agency

Chapter 1

The Hoover Elementary School Library looked like most other school libraries. The shelves were short so the younger kids could reach all of the books. There were signs reminding readers to "Please Stay Quiet". The librarian sat at a big desk by the door where she could check out books and see the Art tables in the middle of the room. However, Madison Lively loved the room at the back of the library. They kept the internet computers in that room.

Madison loved working on computers. She had completed every program the library owned by the time she finished second grade. Now two years later, she was the only fourth grader that could write her own program. She loved making games for her friends. Usually, they were math or spelling games. Sometimes, she made silly games like shooting aliens or treasure hunting.

Now that she was a fourth grader, Madison had earned internet privileges. She visited popular sites like MillerWords.com and even helped her mother with online banking. With her mother's permission, Madison had set up automatic payment for her mother on all of the family bills. Normally, Madison was helpful and always did the right thing.

Today was different. Today, Madison came to the library on a mission. Most days, she stayed after school to study or work on the computer. No one suspected why she was here today. She knew Mrs. Octavo, the librarian, would not bother her in the computer room.

Mr. Crews was the new fourth grade geography teacher. He started right after Winter Break and still could not remember most of the students' names. He came from the high school, so all of his work was harder than the other fourth grade teacher's assignments. His year-end final would be the hardest of all. That was why Madison was here today.

She knew the test would be difficult. No student would be able to pass it. Madison decided to help all of the fourth graders. She wanted to change the test so everyone could get a good grade. Madison knew it was wrong. She felt Mr. Crews was more wrong. He made the test too hard.

It was easy for Madison to access the school website. Then she found Mr. Crews' saved files. She opened the test document. Madison read the questions. She did not know the answer to any of the questions on the first page. Then she saw he made it ten pages long!

"What kind of teacher makes a ten page test?" she asked herself.

Madison started by deleting five pages. Then she quickly started changing the remaining questions. What was the Gross National Product of Zambia? Madison wondered if even Mr. Crews knew that answer. It did not take her long to change the test. She saved the file and closed it. She hoped Mr. Crews would not look at it until it was too late. She knew the volunteers in the front office printed the tests. Mr. Crews probably would not look at it until test day.

She felt relieved. Madison had never hacked a website before. How easily she did it surprised her. She started to close her internet browser. Then she had an idea. She wanted to help all of the students. She wanted every kid at Hoover Elementary to take home a good report card.

Madison looked over her shoulder. She could see Mrs. Octavo sitting at her desk. The nice old woman quietly read a magazine. She could not guess what Madison planned to do. This made Madison feel guilty. She never cheated on a test before. She never lied or stole anything. What was she thinking?

She almost closed her browser again. Then she made a decision. She wanted to help all those kids that could not help themselves. She wanted to be a hero. She wanted to give everyone straight A's!

Madison quickly wrote a short program. The program automatically changed every student's grades. From Kindergarten to Fifth grade, all the B's, C's, D's and a few F's suddenly changed to

4

A's. School would be over in two weeks. Now it did not matter how difficult the final tests were. Every kid would take home his or her best grade card ever. Every kid would get to go out for pizza and ice cream. Every parent would celebrate.

Part of Madison's heart knew it was wrong. A bigger part of her heart was proud. While thinking about this, she did not notice the new flashing icon on her screen until now. The icon said one word: TRACKING. Madison clicked it. The program opened and showed a map of the world. The map changed to the United States. Then it zoomed to Marcelene, her hometown. Then it changed again. She recognized the address. The map zoomed in on her elementary school!

"What's happening?" she said aloud.

Madison turned around to see if Mrs. Octavo heard her. She saw the librarian talking to two men in suits. Mrs. Octavo pointed at the computer room. This scared Madison. How could the men know what she did? How could anyone get here that fast?

She deleted her files off the computer. She grabbed her small backpack. She immediately ducked down and crawled out the door. She made it safely behind the Biography section. A moment later, the two men walked into the computer room. They looked surprised to find it empty. One of the men checked Madison's computer. The other one started whispering into his watch. Who are these men, she thought? They must be government agents.

Madison knew they were looking for her. Now she felt really bad about what she did. She wished it had never happened. She started to sneak toward the back door. All she had to do was get outside, then she could run home. She almost made it to the door, but bumped into a rack of comic books. A few fell to the floor.

"Madison Lively!" said a loud voice.

She turned around to see the agents looking right at her.

"Stop right there!" said the agent.

Madison was too scared.

She ran.

She ran out the back door. She ran across the playground to the grassy field.

Suddenly, something knocked the wind out of her. Someone hit her hard. They crashed to the ground. Madison rolled over. She looked into the face of a ten-year-old boy.

"Hi, I'm Josh," he said. "You're in big trouble."

Chapter 2

Joshua St. Vincent was a star athlete. He played flag-football and baseball. He took karate and fencing lessons. He was only ten years old, but he was the most popular kid in school.

He liked people calling him Josh. And he liked going to George Washington Elementary. Every day, he walked in the front door and saw his picture in the trophy case. Josh did not like to lose.

Today was no different from any other. He had a three-egg omelet with toast and cereal for breakfast. Josh liked food. After twenty minutes of combing his brown hair, he left for school. He went to class and had a gourmet, homemade salad for lunch. Josh liked good nutrition. After school, he walked to the baseball field.

Josh was a B-average student. All of his teachers liked him. He sat in the back of the class, but he did not cause trouble. He turned his homework in on time, every day. He liked school well enough, but liked sports more.

There were only three more weeks of school. When school let out, Josh would spend the entire day at the baseball field. Baseball was the best. He believed no other sport in the world compared to baseball. He only played flag-football in the winter to stay healthy.

Josh had his own wooden baseball bat. His grandpa carved it for him from a two-hundred-year-old maple tree. His grandpa lived on a farm and one day lightning struck the old tree. A huge branch broke off and his grandpa used that to make the bat. His grandpa was a very talented wood-worker. He even made their kitchen table.

Josh carried his bat with him everywhere. He slept with it. He even named it Thunder because of the storm. His grandpa carved the name into the thick part of the bat. Everyone knew it was special and no one asked to borrow it. No one wanted to be blamed if it cracked.

Josh got to the baseball field by three o'clock. Practice did not officially start until four o'clock. Josh would run the bases until his teammates got there. Then he would practice pitching. The team had one other pitcher, but Josh never missed. He would throw the same every time.

Whoosh. Strike.

Josh picked up a ball from the bag by his feet.

Whoosh. Strike.

Josh picked up another ball.

Whoosh. Strike.

"You're out," Josh said in his head.

Josh could throw nine strikes in a row. Every pitch was a fastball, even fast for his age. However, Josh did not know how to through any other kind of pitch. He had heard of curveballs and sliders, but could not learn it. Still, all he needed was his fastball. No other ten-year-old could hit his fastball.

The two-hour practice went by quickly. Josh hit several home runs. He took turns pitching and playing first base. When practice was over, most of the boys left right away. A few stayed to play catch before they had to leave for dinner.

That is when the helicopter came.

It seemed like the huge machine did not make any noise. Josh did not hear it until it was directly over the field. He felt the wind from its propellers first. Then he could hear the foop, foop, foop of the fast spinning blades.

The all black helicopter slowly landed next to the pitcher's mound. The last of Josh's friends ran home. Josh stayed. He was curious.

A man in a suit stepped out of the helicopter. He looked like a secret agent. He walked crouched over as if he was scared of the propeller. He came straight to Josh.

"Joshua St. Vincent?" he asked.

"Maybe," Josh said.

The man grabbed Josh by the shoulder.

"Come with me," he said.

"My mom told me never talk to strangers," said Josh.

He swung his bat, Thunder, and hit the man on the back of the leg. The man fell over. Then two more men jumped out of the helicopter. They came running. Josh ran from home plate toward the dugout. He could either go through the dugout or climb the fence.

Josh decided to climb the fence. As he reached the top, one of the agents grabbed the back of his shirt. The agent pulled him off the fence. Josh rolled on the ground and stood up quickly.

He was not afraid of these men as long as he had Thunder. He swung the bat hard. He almost hit one of them in the stomach. The two agents jumped back. Josh turned to run into the outfield.

The first agent with the hurt leg blocked his path. Josh pulled a baseball out of his backpack. He threw the ball. It was a perfect strike. It hit the agent directly on the forehead.

Before Josh could start running again, the other two agents grabbed him. The first agent got up. He limped to Josh. Josh could see the red bump swelling on his forehead. The agent took Josh's bat and bag.

They carried him over by the helicopter. With the engine off, the blades finally stopped spinning.

A tall man stepped out. His suit looked nicer than the other agents' suits. Also, he seemed to be older. Josh thought the man spent more time combing his hair than he did himself. The man looked serious. The sound of his voice made him seem even more serious.

"My name is Mr. Crux," he said.

Josh notice the man had silver eyes.

"You have been recruited for a very special program," said Mr. Crux.

"Why me?" asked Josh.

"Because of your athletic abilities," answered Mr. Crux. "You are very talented for your age."

"What's the program?" asked Josh.

"I will tell you more later. First, we have to talk to your parents. Then we have to go get your partner," said Mr. Crux.

"Oh yeah, where's my partner?" asked Josh.

"At Hoover Elementary School," said Mr. Crux. "Her name is Madison Lively."

Chapter 3

"Sorry," said Josh.

"Sorry for what?" asked Madison.

"Sorry for knocking you down back at your school," said Josh.

Madison smiled at the boy holding his baseball bat. Then she looked out the window of the airplane. She did not know if they were flying over Arizona or New Mexico. She could only see a lot of desert.

She wanted to remind Josh that it happened two days ago. She could not believe it. It had already been two days since they caught her at school. Why did he wait so long to apologize? She realized this was the first time they had been alone together.

The tall, frightening Mr. Crux had been with them every minute. They went from her school straight to her house. They rode in a limousine. Madison had never done that before.

Mr. Crux told her they specially chose her. He told her mother it was a summer camp for computers. She thought her mother agreed to Mr. Crux's plan too easy. She let Madison leave school two weeks early. She let her go on a plane with a stranger. There must have been something secret on the letter Mr. Crux gave to her mother.

She packed some clothes while her mother made dinner. The two of them ate quietly.

"Your father would be so proud of you," said her mother, finally.

They did not talk about her father very often. He had been gone so long. She was excited.

"Do you think so?" Madison asked.

"Yes," said her mother. "I am too. I am going to miss you."

They hugged. Madison thought about how lonely her mother would be while she was gone. Madison promised herself to ask about her father when the time was right.

Now, she was on a private plane. She and Josh were the only two passengers. They each had their own flight attendant. The man and woman brought them lunch and made sure they had plenty of juice and water. Madison had never been on a plane before.

It excited her so much and made her very nervous. Mr. Crux told her very little about the program. Josh did not seem to know much about it either.

Still, Josh seemed nice. He was a cute boy with dimples. She thought he might spend more time on his hair than she did. Every strand of his dark brown hair stayed perfectly in place with gel. He looked like a secret agent when he put on his sunglasses. Of course, secret agents never wore jeans and a t-shirt.

Finally, the plane started to land. All she could see in every direction was sand. They were in the middle of nowhere. There was a small hangar and a fuel pump for the plane. She saw only one other building. It looked small like a tool shed.

The pilot waved bye. Then the male flight attendant led them to the tool shed. They went through the creaky wooden door and stood in front of an elevator. The attendant pushed a button and then went back to the plane.

When the elevator doors opened, Mr. Crux surprised Madison and Josh. He stood inside the elevator.

"Please, get in. We have much to discuss," he said.

Josh went in first. Not very polite, thought Madison. She stepped in next. She saw only two buttons, up and down. Mr. Crux pushed the down button. The doors closed and they went down. They went down very fast. Madison thought her feet might rise off the floor because they dropped so fast.

After two minutes, the doors opened onto a long, white hallway. Mr. Crux led them silently down the hall. The hall ended at a circular room with ten doors. Madison saw that none of the doors had a handle. They did not even have a control pad like in the movies.

Mr. Crux must have seen her puzzled expression.

He said, "The doors have genetic sensors. They only open when they scan your DNA. Totally secure. If you are not in the database, the door will not open. We already loaded your samples into the database."

Josh stepped up to one of the steel doors. Madison could hear a soft hum. Then the edges of the doorframe turned green and the door opened. She could see a man sitting at a desk in front of a small platform.

"That is the teleportation room. You'll be using that later," said Mr. Crux. He ushered Josh away from the door and it slipped closed.

"Over here are your personal rooms," he said. Mr. Crux pointed at two doors on the other side of the circle.

Madison wanted to know more about the teleportation room.

"You have a transporter?" she asked. "Like in Star Trek?"

"Not just one transporter," said Mr. Crux. He smiled, but it looked creepy. "We have teleportation rooms in every base in almost every country in the world."

Madison could not believe it. How could they keep something like that a secret?

"What's in this room?" asked Josh.

"That's the armory," said Mr. Crux.

"Cool," said Josh. "Weapons."

Mr. Crux led them to the center door. After the scan, the frame turned green and the door opened. They stepped through onto a balcony. Madison could not believe her eyes. The room was huge. People worked on dozens of computers. Giant screens on the walls showed maps and videos. Some of the videos showed kids her age doing acrobatics or weapon training. People went in every direction, all very busy.

Madison and Josh turned to look at Mr. Crux.

He said, "Welcome to Small World Global Protection Agency."

Chapter 4

Josh spent the next several days exploring the headquarters. He really liked the weapon's room. However, he spent most of his time in the training room and the dining room.

He and Madison trained together. He practiced karate and started learning Kung Fu. Madison learned gymnastics. It made Josh laugh when her long auburn curls hung in her face each time she did a handstand. Her freckles stood out even more when the blood rushed to her head in that pose.

Mr. Crux spent time with them in the conference room. He told them about Small World Global Protection Agency.

"Sometimes, there are missions which no adult can do. Sometimes, only a child can save the day," he said. "Small World has a special purpose. Not only do we fight the bad guys. We have to protect history. We have to educate people on their own culture. We carefully select two children in every country of the world. These two children are very talented and very smart. They have to know everything about their country and share it with the world."

Mr. Crux slapped two American History books on the table. He slid them across to Josh and Madison.

"Homework?" said Josh.

"Is there a problem, Agent St. Vincent?" asked Mr. Crux.

Josh was not a big fan of homework. He decided he should not say that to Mr. Crux.

Mr. Crux said, "Not only are you Protection Agents, but you are cultural ambassadors. You have to know everything about your country. You have to learn it and share it. Knowledge is your best weapon."

Josh and Madison spent the next several weeks training and studying. Josh started by learning about George Washington, since that was the name of his school. He learned the difference between George Washington and George Washington Carver. He could not decide who was more amazing. They both did great things.

He saw Madison spend a lot of time in the control room. She was good with computers, but he was not. She studied online history while he was stuck with dusty books.

Josh was better at athletics than Madison. She learned gymnastics quickly. Still, with his expert trainer, he mastered Kung Fu even faster. Next, he could not decide whether to learn Native American wrestling or Brazilian Capoeira.

"What's Capo-whatever?" asked Madison.

"Look it up in the encyclopedia," said Josh. "That's what I did."

They ate healthy meals together and trained together. Soon, they were becoming good friends.

Mr. Crux said, "You have to rely on your partner. You have to know their next thought. You have to know he or she will be their when you need them most. Even when you are outnumbered, you cannot lose with your partner."

Josh enjoyed his new life. They even had a pitching machine so he could practice baseball. He still slept with his bat, Thunder. He took Thunder to the training room to use with the pitching machine. He hit baseballs for thirty minutes every day. His martial arts master even taught him different ways to use Thunder aside from baseball.

One day, Mr. Crux called Josh and Madison to the conference room. He had a folder for each of them. He also had a slide projector set up on the table. When they took their seats, Mr. Crux pushed a button on the remote control and the lights went out.

The slide projector came to life. The first image showed a map of the country of Australia.

"This is your first assignment," said Mr. Crux.

"What? We have to save Australia?" said Josh. He thought he was being funny.

"No," said Mr. Crux. "You have to save the world." Mr. Crux did not look amused.

Mr. Crux clicked a button and the slide picture changed. The screen filled with a photo of a very pretty girl. Josh thought she looked familiar, but he did not know any teenagers.

"I know her," said Madison. "That's Ja-Naya. She's Australia's number one pop singer right now."

"That's correct, Agent Lively," said Mr. Crux. "She is your mission."

Josh looked at the picture again. He saw her make-up and shiny blonde hair. He wondered how she could be a villain.

Mr. Crux said, "You two are going to pose as brother and sister. We have arranged for you to win the Spend the Week with Ja-Naya contest. You have to get close to her so you can get close to her manager."

"So her manager is the real target," said Madison.

This relieved Josh because he already started to have a crush on Ja-Naya. He did not want her to be bad.

"Mr. Feeble Bix is her manager and producer," said Mr. Crux.

The slide changed to reveal an enormous man with a bald head. He had a huge mole on his left cheek and his two big teeth on top and bottom were gold. The man held a huge sandwich in one hand and Ja-Naya's contract in the other.

"Bix is taking over Ja-Naya's contract now that she has reached the top of the Australian music charts. He has arranged for her new album to have a premier around the world on the same day."

"Lots of singers do that," said Josh.

"But never at the same time," said Mr. Crux. "The CD is going to be released at the exact same moment all over the world. People will be lining up in the middle of the night and the middle of the day. The strange thing is that no one has heard any of the songs."

"That's right. You can't even find it leaked on the internet," said Madison. Then she looked embarrassed. "I mean for someone that would do something dishonest like that."

Mr. Crux looked disapproving for a moment. Then he said, "We do not know why he has arranged the release like this. That is what we want you to discover."

Mr. Crux clicked the next slide. This picture showed two of the friendliest looking kids Josh could imagine. They both dressed in tan shirts and matching tan shorts with lots of pockets. The boy had a funny looking cowboy hat with one side folded up. The girl held a boomerang.

"Some other Small World agents?" asked Madison.

"Right. These are your contacts. Mick and Kim," said Mr. Crux. "They will teach you everything you need to know about Australia and Ja-Naya."

Josh got excited about going to Australia. He had never been outside of the United States before. It seemed like a fun vacation. It did not worry him at all about Feeble Bix or any possible danger.

"Get what you need from the armory. I recommend snake repellant. Then head to the teleportation room," said Mr. Crux.

Josh had not thought about the teleportation room since the first day. This made him nervous, but Madison looked excited.

Chapter 5

Madison quickly filled a backpack from the armory. She could not wait to try the teleporter. She rushed into the teleportation room. She knew the agent working at the desk. His code name was Eleven, but everybody called him Lev.

"Hi Lev," said Madison.

"Good afternoon, Agent Lively," said Lev.

"You can call me Madison," she said.

"Afraid I can't, miss. You're the reason the rest of us are here. Mr. Crux gave strict instructions to treat you both with respect. You see, you're the boss," said Lev.

This made Madison feel funny. She could not imagine all these people and technology were here only for her and Josh.

"But aren't there any other agents?" she asked.

Lev said, "Only you two. When you get older you move on to other things, as did the previous agents."

"Like what?" asked Josh. He walked in the room still stuffing snake repellant into his bag.

"Like MIT or the CIA," said Lev. "You two are destined for great things." Lev smiled big and pushed his thick glasses back up his nose. His glasses constantly slid down his nose.

Madison stepped up on the platform. She believed she was ready to go. She noticed Josh did not seem as excited.

"What's wrong, Josh?" she asked.

"I'm not too sure about this teleportation," Josh said.

Madison patted him on the shoulder.

"Don't worry," she said. "All it does is break us into atoms and beam us through the air on radio waves."

"Actually, that's not exactly correct," said Lev. "These days, we digitally map you at the sub-particle level. Then you are disintegrated. We transmit your template over the internet to the receiving computer. That computer reads the blueprint. It uses localized atmospheric particles to reconstruct you. Digital is way better than analog radio waves."

Josh looked like it might make him sick.

"Don't worry. It's perfectly safe," said Mr. Crux as he walked in the room.

Mr. Crux ushered Josh onto the platform. Then he signaled Lev to transmit.

Mr. Crux said, "Oh, be sure to hold your breath."

Madison quickly sucked in a gasp.

Josh tried to say, "Why?"

ZAP.

Suddenly, Mr. Crux and Lev were gone. Lev had been replaced by a young woman. Madison let out her breath. She turned to Josh.

He finished saying, "Why?" Then he sucked for air and fainted.

Madison knelt beside him and two other kids rushed into the room. Madison recognized Mick and Kim from their picture.

"Don't worry. He'll be alright," said Kim.

"Yeah. Happens to lotsa cobbers their first time," said Mick.

Josh sat up. He shook his head.

"That wasn't funny," said Josh.

Mick helped him up and then gave him a big hug.

"G'day," said Mick. "Welcome to Small World Australia."

Kim led the group out of the teleporter room. They stood in a circular room exactly like the one at their base. The whole place seemed to be the same, except for the people. Madison wondered if they really did transport. She still thought it was only possible in science fiction.

They walked down the hallway toward the elevator. Mick stood in front of the door for the scan. Then he stepped out of the way to let Madison and Kim on first.

"Now we're a bit back of beyond, so we have plenty of catching up time," said Mick. The elevator started its long upward trip.

"Where are we?" asked Josh.

The elevator doors opened. Madison looked out across an immense flat brown land. In the distance, she saw an enormous rock sticking out of the ground. She knew from pictures that it was the famous Ayers Rock. The giant sandstone rock is all that is left of a prehistoric mountain range.

Mick opened his arms to the morning sun. He said, "We're in the Outback, mate!"

Madison almost could not believe it. The teleporter instantly shot them to the other side of the world.

"We have a fair bit of a walkabout if we're going to have you in Sydney tomorrow morn," said Mick.

"But aren't we in the Northern Territory?" asked Madison.

"Good on ya, Madi," said Kim. "Think of the US of A. If we were in your Kansas, we have to get to Florida in less than a day."

"But we ain't got none of them girly alligators here, mate," said Mick. "Your Florida gators take one look at our crocs and they'd crawl right back in their eggshells."

Mick took his hat off the hook by the door. Josh tried not to laugh.

"Why's your hat bent like that?" Josh asked.

"First, yank, this ain't no hat. It's a slouch. My pa was a digger and it was his. He left it to me," said Mick.

"Digger?" asked Josh.

"We call soldiers that," said Kim. "The slouch shows a history of Aussie pride and confidence."

Kim pointed to a mud covered Range Rover. A dark-skinned man sat behind the wheel. He cranked the engine when they walked toward him.

"Is he an aborigine?" asked Madison.

"Right you are again," said Kim. "That's Matari. He's going to drive us to Sydney. You didn't really think we were going to walk?"

"This will give us plenty of time to talk about that larrikin Feeble Bix before he puts that beaut Ja-Naya up a gum tree," said Mick.

When they were in the truck, Matari sped away. The Range Rover scattered a mob of Kangaroo. Hundreds of paws rumbled the ground as they jumped clear of the truck.

Chapter 6

The children talked about their mission while Matari drove them across the country. Josh enjoyed the different way the Australians talked.

Kim talked about Feeble Bix and his record company, Big Bix Records. They talked about him being so rich.

"But no one knows how he got all of his money," said Kim.

"Ja-Naya is his first star?" asked Madison.

"That's right," said Mick. "He's never had a successful singer before."

Josh wanted to know more about Feeble Bix, but he was tired. He thought it must already be night back in the United States. He wished he learned more about Time

Zones when he was in school. Luckily, he had Madison for a partner. She seemed like she knew a lot about those kinds of things. Josh noticed Madison yawning. This made him yawn too. Soon, they both fell asleep.

When Josh woke up, they were driving through a huge city. This looked very different from the outback. They drove past skyscrapers and over waterways. Josh could not believe how many seafood restaurants he could see.

Kim said, "There's the Sydney Convention Centre."

They crossed another big bridge.

"And over there's the Sydney Aquarium," said Mick.

Madison looked very excited to see everything. Josh felt amazed by all of the towering hotels. Mick pointed to a three-story sandstone building.

"That's the Customs House," said Mick.

"What do they do there?" asked Josh.

"It's a library now," said Kim.

"Before that, it was like an office for all of the shipping in the harbor," said Mick. "They collected taxes for all the things brought by the boats. Sailors had to get permission from the Customs House to bring their goods and animals to or from Australia."

"The building has been there since 1845," said Kim.

"Wow, that's old," said Madison.

Then the Customs House disappeared out of sight. They now passed a huge park. Josh could see lush green trees of all types.

"What's this place?" Josh asked.

"That's the Royal Botanic Gardens," said Kim. "It leads right up to where we are going."

"Where are we going?" asked Madison.

Josh could see a huge building with strange curved roofs.

"Welcome to Bennelong Point," said Mick. "Home of the world famous Sydney Opera House and our destination."

Josh could see that it was definitely not a house. He counted three different buildings. They each had the same type of roof. He thought they looked like giant clamshells. He had seen this building in many movies and TV shows.

"Ja-Naya is going to give a concert to celebrate the release of her album," said Mick.

"She's rehearsing in the concert hall now. That's in the biggest building," said Kim.

Matari stopped the truck. The kids got out and Josh was amazed by the size of the buildings.

"Did you know there are six different size theatres inside plus the Forecourt for outdoor shows?" asked Kim.

Josh did not know that. The movies always made him think it was one big theatre. It excited him to actually go inside the famous building.

Kim gave a lanyard to both him and Madison. He hung the strap around his neck. The badge attached to it said "Winner" on one side. On the other side, he saw his picture and the words "Spend the Week with Ja-Naya".

Kim and Mick had badges too. They went up to one of the side doors. They all showed their badges to a man in a suit. Josh thought he must work for Big Bix Security.

The man led them inside the Opera House. They went through several back halls. They passed into a dark room and Josh could hear loud music. The sound shook the floor under his feet. He looked toward the bright light at the other side of the room. He could see people on stage.

"We're backstage!" exclaimed Josh.

A woman wearing a headset microphone said, "Shhhhhhh." She quickly walked away looking at her clipboard with a flashlight.

The security guard put his hand in front of them. Apparently, he wanted them to wait. The guard walked over to another man and whispered in his ear. Josh thought he, Madison, Mick and Kim could easily fit inside the rotund man's purple suit. Josh knew this had to be Feeble Bix. Josh watched Bix suck the meat off a fried chicken leg in one bite.

After the guard finished whispering, Bix barely turned his head to look at the kids.

"Alright," Bix said in a booming voice.

The music stopped instantly. Everyone on stage must have been able to hear Bix.

Bix said, "Everyone, take a fifteen minute break."

The people on stage walked into the backstage area. Josh watched musicians pass him headed straight for the food table. Josh saw a delicious looking mix of sandwiches, snacks and drinks.

The choir members came next. Then at least twenty back-up dancers followed them.

A tall girl with two longs pigtails walked off the stage last. Her blonde hair was braided with five strands in each pigtail. At the bottom, a light blue flower held the two pigtails together. The color of the flower matched the color of her eyes.

Josh remembered the picture of Ja-Naya back at headquarters. He thought she was pretty at that time. Now he thought she was beautiful. In fact, he thought she must be the most beautiful fourteen-year-old in the world. He definitely had a crush on her now. He could feel his ears and cheeks turning red.

Mick introduced himself. So did Kim and Madison. Josh took his turn.

"Um, my name is, um, I forgot," said Josh. Ja-Naya made Josh nervous, so the only thing he could say was, "I like hamburgers."

Ja-Naya smiled at him. Then she went back on stage to rehearse.

Chapter 7

They left the concert hall. Ja-Naya still had a lot of rehearsing to do. Matari drove them to their hotel. The size of the Shangri La Hotel impressed Madison. She thought she might be able to see all of Sydney from the top.

When they got to their room on the twentieth floor, it did not disappoint. She could see the Opera House from there. She could also see far off over the bay. She could see many boats of every type. Many of them carried products to and from other countries. Still, many others held happy families on vacations. She guessed the people that owned the big yachts had to be very rich.

Josh turned on the giant flat-screen television. Madison was glad he was acting normal again. She thought he must have a serious crush on Ja-Naya. She knew Ja-Naya was much older than they were. That girl probably liked boys her own age.

She watched Josh rapidly change the channels. He could not decide on a show.

"What are you looking for?" asked Madison.

"Baseball," said Josh.

"Crikey!" said Mick. "You won't find baseball here."

Mick grabbed the remote control. He changed the channel to a sport Madison had never seen. Apparently, neither had Josh.

"What's this?" Josh exclaimed.

"THIS is cricket," Mick said proudly. "It's only the most popular sport in the world."

"Right after football," said Kim.

"I like football," said Josh.

"Sorry mate," said Kim. "I'm not talking about American Football. I'm talking about real football. You yanks call it soccer."

Mick looked as if he did not like being teased by Kim. Josh looked confused. Madison did not care either way. She did not like sports. All she wanted to do was check her email. Luckily, the room was so fancy it came with a computer. While she checked for messages from her mother, Mick and Josh watched cricket.

"It looks a lot like baseball," said Josh.

"Except there are eleven players on each side," said Mick.

"Well, there's the pitcher," said Josh.

Mick said, "He's called the bowler. He's trying to break the wicket."

"That must be those sticks behind the batter," said Josh.

"Right you are, mate," said Mick. He looked excited that Josh was learning the game.

When the boys started cheering, Madison became interested. She decided to search for the International Cricket Council on the internet to learn more.

After the game, everyone had supper. Next they had to talk about the mission. Kim spread a map of Sydney across the table. Madison quickly spotted their hotel, the Opera House and even the Customs House. Kim pointed to a spot close to their hotel.

"This is the Big Bix Records warehouse," said Kim. "This is where all of Ja-Naya's new albums are waiting to be shipped."

Madison guessed, "So, we have to go in there?"

"We have to find out what's so important about those compact discs," said Kim. "And we have to do it before any of them leave the country."

The kids checked their backpacks. Madison decided she would not need the snake repellent in the city. She left it on the table. Then they left the hotel.

The warehouse was in walking distance. Soon, Madison and her friends stood in the side alley. Big Bix security guards watched the front entrance. Madison did not feel like they were safely hidden. Even at night, Sydney was so full of lights that the alley did not have many shadows.

"Alright, girl, it's your turn," said Mick.

It took a moment for Madison to realize he was talking to her and not Kim.

"What do I have to do?" asked Madison.

"Use your gymnastics to get up there," said Kim. She pointed to a second story window.

Madison looked around the alley. The fire escape ladder seemed too high to reach from the ground. Madison quickly ran toward the building next door. She jumped as high as she could straight at the wall. She stuck her feet out in front of her. When her feet hit the wall, she kicked as hard as she could. This made her do a back flip right over the heads of her friends. Madison flew through the air. At the last second, she grabbed the bottom rung of the ladder with one hand.

Josh ran beneath Madison. He acted like he would catch her if she fell. Madison pulled herself up the ladder. From the top, she lowered the ladder for everyone else. Kim and Josh climbed up next to her.

"What are you doing, Mick?" asked Josh.

"I'm going to be the lookout," said Mick.

Madison, Josh and Kim walked up the fire escape to the second floor. Luckily, someone left the window unlocked. They snuck inside. Madison could not believe how many cases of CD's filled the room. The rows of boxes seemed as big as the inside of the concert hall where Ja-Naya rehearsed.

They climbed down to the warehouse floor. Madison kept watching for the security guards. The possibility of being caught scared her. Kim pulled out a pocketknife and opened one of the boxes. It was full of CD cases with Ja-Naya's picture on the front of each. Madison thought they looked like normal albums. Kim opened one of the discs.

"Here, give this a scan," said Kim.

Madison pulled a very small notebook computer out of her backpack. The computer was not much bigger than the disc. She slid the disc in the side and quickly scanned it. The little computer impressed her with a fast scan and report.

"No viruses or worms," said Madison.

Madison did not notice Josh open another CD. He put the disc in his mp3 player and put the headphones in his ears. Madison's computer gave her a warning about the disc. She turned to Josh right as he pushed the play button.

"Wait Josh!" screamed Madison.

As soon as the music started, Josh's face turned pale white. His eyes started flashing red in tune with the music. Madison realized the music hypnotized him.

Kim pulled the headphones out of their plug. Josh quickly turned back to normal.

"So that's his plan," said Madison. "Feeble Bix is trying to take over the world.

He's going to do it with a program hidden on these discs."

"If everyone in the world starts listening to it at the same time then there will be no one to turn the music off," said Kim.

"We have the proof," said Josh. "Let's get out of here."

They turned to leave and met face to face with five security guards. Madison thought they must have heard her yell at Josh. Now they had no escape.

Chapter 8

Josh looked at the five guards. He quickly reached over his shoulder to grab his bat, Thunder. He found nothing there! He yanked off his backpack only to realize he did not have Thunder. Now he remembered leaving the baseball bat on the hotel bed.

"Um, I think we're in trouble," said Josh.

"Run," shouted Kim.

The three kids each ran in different directions. The guards did not know what to do. They looked at each other and then started chasing.

Josh saw Madison climb up on top of the crates. Then she did a no-handed cartwheel over one of the guard's heads. She landed on top of the next row of crates and kept running.

Josh felt a hand pulling at the back of his shirt. One of the guards almost caught him! Josh shook loose and took off down one of the many aisles. He kept turning at each opening. He hoped to lose the guards, but did not know a way out of the warehouse.

Finally, Josh came to a wall. He could only turn left or right. He turned right and came to another wall. He thought this warehouse was like a maze. He realized he must be in the back corner of the building. Josh turned right again. Now he was face-to-face with the guard that had been chasing him!

Josh ran toward the guard. He imagined himself playing baseball. In his mind, he tried to steal home plate. He did a perfect slide on the smooth concrete floor. Josh slid right between the guard's legs. He jumped up and took off running.

Suddenly, another guard appeared from a side aisle. Now he had two guards chasing him. They sure looked mad, Josh thought. He did not let that slow him down. He guessed he was heading toward the front of the building. He planned to run straight out the front door.

If Josh got outside, he did not know what to do next. He wondered if he should call the police. Would they believe this story from a ten-year-old boy? Then he remembered Madison and Kim. He was so worried about not being caught that he forgot about the girls. He hoped they already got away.

Passing the last row of boxes answered his question. There was a wide-open space between the crates and the front door. To one side, Josh noticed a small office. All five Big Bix security guards stood between him and the front door. One guard held Madison and another held Kim. The guards gripped them tightly by the shoulders so that the girls could not escape.

The fifth guard held a canvas sack. The sack seemed to be squirming. The guard dumped out the contents of the sack. Josh jumped back at the sight of an Australian Tiger Snake. Now he wished Madison packed the snake repellent.

Josh raised his hands. He said, "I surrender."

The office door opened. A man stood inside the doorway. A cloud of smoke spilled out, hiding the man's face. Still, Josh knew who it was. He thought no amount of smoke could hide this man's giant body. The overly round Feeble Bix stepped out of the office.

"Well, well, well," said Bix. "What have we got here?"

Bix turned to Josh first. He leaned in close. Josh could see bits of greasy food stuck in the man's teeth.

"Seems our little prize winners got a bit excited," said Bix. "Now, I was gonna make sure you could listen to the music. But you had to go and spoil the surprise early."

Feeble Bix took a step backward. Josh thought he was going to step on the poisonous snake. Instead, the snake wrapped around Bix's ankle and slowly wound its way up the man's leg. When the snake slid behind Bix's neck, he patted it on the head.

Bix talked to the snake with a baby voice. "Come here my pet. Did the meany-weany kiddies fwighten you? It's ok. Daddy woves you."

Josh could not help it. He burst with laughter. Apparently, Bix did not like Josh's response.

"Get these kids to the concert hall," yelled Bix.

The guards dragged the kids outside to a waiting limousine. They forced them into the car. As the last guard shoved Josh inside, Josh noticed something at the corner of the building. It was Mick!

This excited Josh. A minute ago, he thought he was going to be snake food. Now he thought Mick could rescue them. Before Mick could do anything, the limousine drove away from the warehouse.

Josh wanted to tell Madison and Kim that he saw Mick. He could not figure out how to do it without the guards hearing him. Instead, he sat in silence all the way back to the Sydney Opera House.

Josh could not believe all the people waiting there. Then he remembered Ja-Naya's concert. She was going to sing tonight to celebrate her new CD. It looked like a Sold Out crowd.

The guards led Josh, Madison and Kim in the same side door as the first time. This time they were prisoners, not contest winners. The guards took them up several flights of stairs, then onto a narrow walkway.

Josh could see lights coming from below and hear music. He looked over the rail. They were high above the stage. He could see

Ja-Naya warming up with her band. They looked like ants from way up here.

The guards tied all three kids with ropes.

"What are you planning to do with us?" asked Kim.

"We wait for Mr. Bix," said the guard. "But he'll probably tell us to drop you off somewhere." Then the guard looked over the rail and laughed.

Chapter 9

It felt like a long time. Madison wondered if Mr. Bix forgot about them. She waited as Ja-Naya cleared the stage. Soon, crowds of people began filling the concert hall.

Madison thought she should have been scared at a time like this. Then she thought maybe that is why she was chosen for the Global Protection Agency. Guards tied them up high above a stage in Australia. Madison was not scared; she was excited. She hoped Mick was working to help them. However, she had one other secret.

The guards did not check her watch! Madison wiggled her arms until she could reach her watch with the opposite hand. She twisted the dial. Suddenly, a small laser burst out. The tiny beam started burning through the ropes immediately. Madison knew it would only be a matter of minutes until she was loose.

Down below, the crowd sounded ready. They started cheering as Ja-Naya took the stage. The guards came over to the rail to have a peek. Madison decided to stop her laser in case one of them noticed.

The music blasted out of the giant speakers on the stage. Madison could even feel it vibrating the walkway way up here. Despite being prisoners, she enjoyed the music. Madison liked that all of Ja-Naya's songs were about good things like life, love and nature. It made her sad that Feeble Bix would use such good music to make people into mindless zombies.

Mr. Bix finally arrived. Madison saw him reach the top of the steps at the far end of the walkway. He looked very out of breath after climbing so many stairs. Mr. Bix had to turn sideways to squeeze between the narrow rails. Madison could even feel the walkway sway under his extra weight.

Down below, Ja-Naya kept singing. Madison hoped the singer was not a part of Bix's evil plan. Madison was sure Ja-Naya did not know about the hidden program or about the prisoners high above her.

Mr. Bix looked at the three kids. Slimy sweat dripped from his bald head. Madison thought the stairs must have been too much exercise for him. This made her glad that she liked exercise.

"Now, what am I going to do with you lot?" asked Mr. Bix.

"You could let us go," said Josh, with a smile.

Mr. Bix did not like Josh's answer. He poked his thick index finger into Josh's chest.

"If I let you go, it will be right over this rail," said Mr. Bix. "I don't think that's what you had in mind."

Josh's smile disappeared from his face. Madison did not like being up here. She could tell Josh really did not like heights. Josh did not say another word after that.

Then Madison noticed some movement behind Mr. Bix. Hiding at the top of the stairs, she saw Mick. He pointed something at Feeble Bix. Madison thought it looked like a gun. Then she realized it was a special microphone. It was the kind of microphone that could hear people from far away.

Madison knew what she had to do.

"Please Mr. Bix. Please don't hurt us," said Madison. She pretended to be scared. "But if you do, please tell us about your plan."

"That's easy. I'm going to play the new record for you," said Mr. Bix.

"What will that do?" asked Madison. Now she pretended like she did not already know.

"You see, I've hidden a special program on every one of Ja-Naya's CD's," said Feeble Bix. "When that music plays, whoever hears the program will be hypnotized. All over the world, millions of people will instantly become zombies. They will do whatever I tell them. They will force other people to listen to the music. I will be able to walk into banks and take whatever I want. I can take expensive art from famous museums. I will have entire armies at my command. And NO ONE will be able to stop me."

"Well, almost no one," shouted Mick. Madison watched Mick push a button on his microphone. Down below, Ja-Naya's music stopped playing. Feeble Bix's speech replaced the happy sounds. Now everyone knew his evil plan.

Madison quickly activated her laser again. She sliced through her last rope. She turned up the laser and had Josh and Kim free in an instant.

Feeble Bix looked like a scared rabbit. He tried to run, but could only scoot across the walkway. His large belly pressed against the rails. When he made it to the end of the walk, Mick blocked the down stairs. Bix turned and went up one last narrow flight of stairs.

Madison threw their cut ropes at the guards. This slowed the guards down enough for them to get off the catwalk. Kim gave Mick a big hug.

"Where did he go?" asked Josh.

Mick pointed up to a small door. Madison could see a starry sky outside the door. The four kids quickly climbed the stairs.

When they went through the door, Madison had to catch her breath. They found themselves standing on the curved roof of the Sydney Opera House! The ground looked very far below them. Madison saw many police cars approaching the building. She knew Feeble Bix could not get away. Still they had to chase him, so he could not hide.

Bix already headed over the next curved section of roof. Madison did not think he could safely slide down the giant shell. She was right. Feeble Bix had nowhere else to run. He stood at the edge and turned to face the kids. Bix tried to yell at them, but Madison could not hear over the wind and police sirens.

A strong gust of wind rushed past and the kids had to duck down on the roof to keep from losing their balance. When Madison looked up, Feeble Bix was gone. She carefully moved to the edge in time to see Bix falling. He landed in the water of Farm Cove. In a moment, he was surrounded by Water Police boats.

"Can we go back inside now?" asked Josh.

Chapter 10

Josh briefly looked at the Sydney Morning Herald newspaper. The picture showed Feeble Bix in handcuffs. The article said all of the dangerous CD's were being destroyed. There was no mention of Josh or his friends.

"That's ok," said Kim. "We are supposed to be *secret* agents."

Ja-Naya came to visit them at their hotel. She kept thanking them each for helping.

"I would have felt so bad if my music was used to take over the world," said Ja-Naya.

She gave each of them an autographed picture. She also promised to send them her album when it was fixed.

"How about a smacker for a reward?" said Mick. Josh did not know what that meant. When he watched Ja-Naya kiss Mick on the cheek his face turned beet red. He blushed even more when he realized it was his turn. Ja-Naya's lipstick left a print on his cheek.

Matari waited for them at the front of the hotel. He had the engine running. Josh, Madison, Mick and Kim climbed into the Range Rover. They waived bye to Ja-Naya as she was surrounded by fans asking for autographs.

They made the long journey into the outback. Josh watched the scenery of this amazing country. He wished he had a camera. During the journey, they had to stop to change a flat tire. A small river ran alongside the road. Josh got out of the truck to stretch his legs. A crocodile popped up out of the nearby water. Josh jumped back into the truck so fast that he left one of his shoes behind.

When they were back at Mick and Kim's headquarters, they rode the elevator deep underground. The kids all got cleaned up and Josh got a new pair of shoes. They ate lunch together and then decided to go to bed.

Madison suggested they sleep until it was morning back home.

"But it's not even dark yet," said Josh.

"Don't forget about the time change," said Kim. "Your home is several hours behind us."

"You mean ahead, right?" asked Josh.

Madison corrected him. "We crossed the International Date Line to get here."

Time zones always confused Josh. He did not want to think about it after everything else they went through.

They rested for a while and then it was time to go home. Josh and Madison stood on the platform in the transporter room.

"Never thought I'd have a Yank for a cobber," said Mick.

Josh did not understand Mick most of the time. He looked to Kim for a translation.

"He means you guys are his friends," said Kim.

They each took turns hugging each other goodbye. Finally, Kim signaled to the teleporter operator.

"This time, I'll remember to hold my br...." Josh started to say. Before he could finish speaking, the air was sucked out of him.

Josh woke up on the floor of his own teleportation room. Madison knelt by his side and Mr. Crux stood over him. They left the teleportation room. Mr. Crux led them to the main operations room.

Everyone looked busy at his or her computers. Light flashed and phones rang.

"Job well done," said Mr. Crux.

This made Josh feel proud of their mission.

Mr. Crux continued, "You do realize this is only the beginning? Of course, you will get some time off to visit your families. Then we need you back here."

"We have another mission?" asked Madison. She looked as excited as Josh felt.

"Not just one," said Mr. Crux.

He pointed at the screen that covered the entire wall at the far end of the operations room. The screen was as wide as a baseball diamond and stood two stories tall. The different images of security cameras and graphs were replaced with one big image. Soon a map of the world filled the entire screen.

Josh watched as little red lights blinked on all over the map. It seemed that almost every country had its own light. Josh could name most of the countries like Japan, Canada and England. Still, there were many that he did not know.

"The Global Protection Agency has agents like you all over the world," said Mr. Crux. "We cannot rest until all of these lights are off."

"You mean those are all missions?" asked Madison.

"I guess I better start studying geography," said Josh.

Points to Ponder

What is something new that you learned about Australia?

Would you like to visit Australia?

What is one other country you would like to visit?

Would you want to be an International Secret Agent?

Who is your favorite character, Josh or Madison? Why?

44802733R00042

Made in the USA
Middletown, DE
16 June 2017